For Mary Mitchell and Jim Weber, with hugs
—E.S.
For Katrina
—D. A.

Library of Congress Cataloging-in-Publication Data
Spinelli, Eileen.
  Hug a bug / Eileen Spinelli ; illustrated by Dan Andreasen. — 1st ed.
     p.   cm.
  Summary: A simple hug can make anyone, or anything, feel better.
  ISBN 978-0-06-051832-5 (trade bdg.) — ISBN 978-0-06-051833-2 (lib. bdg.)
  [1. Hugging—Fiction. 2. Stories in rhyme.] I. Andreasen, Dan, ill. II. Title.
PZ8.3.S759Hu 2008   2007002987
[E]—dc22   CIP
                                                                              AC

Typography by Jeanne L. Hogle
1 2 3 4 5 6 7 8 9 10
❖
First Edition

EILEEN SPINELLI
Hug a Bug

ILLUSTRATED BY DAN ANDREASEN

HarperCollins*Publishers*

Hug your darling.

Hug the cook.

Hug a painting.

Hug a book.

Hug your pillow.

Hug your pet.

Hug the mailman—
don't forget.

Hug your friend
who's feeling blue.

Hug the firefighter, too.

Hug a teacher.

Hug a bear.

Hug the girl
who cuts
your hair.

Hug a bug—
be gentle, please.

Hug a kitten—
just don't squeeze.

Step right up
and hug that grouch.

Be prepared—
he might say, "Ouch!"

But when you hug that grouch,

he'll see how very sweet
a hug can be.

And he'll start
hugging things
himself—
the cook,

a book from his own shelf.

He'll hug a
waitress,

hug a tree.
He'll join you in this hugging spree.

Hug the dentist.

Hug a clown.

Hug the mayor of your town.

Hug a neighbor passing by.
Hug the whole wide world . . . or try.